HOCKEY SUPER SIX

SHOOTING STARS

BY KEVIN SYLVESTER

Scholastic Canada Ltd.
Toronto New York London Auckland Sydney
Mexico City New Delhi Hong Kong Buenos Aires

Dedicated to everyone who treats their opponents like people: with respect.

Scholastic Canada Ltd.
604 King Street West, Toronto, Ontario M5V 1E1, Canada

Scholastic Inc.
557 Broadway, New York, NY 10012, USA

Scholastic Australia Pty Limited
PO Box 579, Gosford, NSW 2250, Australia

Scholastic New Zealand Limited
Private Bag 94407, Botany, Manukau 2163, New Zealand

Scholastic Children's Books
Euston House, 24 Eversholt Street, London NW1 1DB, UK

www.scholastic.ca

Library and Archives Canada Cataloguing in Publication
Title: Shooting stars / Kevin Sylvester.
Names: Sylvester, Kevin, author, illustrator.
Series: Sylvester, Kevin. Hockey super six.
Description: Series statement: Hockey super six
Identifiers: Canadiana (print) 20210285745 | Canadiana (ebook) 20210285753 |
ISBN 9781443182959 (softcover) | ISBN 9781443194068 (EPUB)
Classification: LCC PS8637.Y42 S56 2022 | DDC jC813/.6—dc23

6 5 4 3 2 1   Printed in Canada 114   22 23 24 25 26

Z!
Z!
Zzz! Zzz!
Zzzzzzz!

CHAPTER ONE

QUIET . . . *TOO* QUIET?

Wait . . . **CHAPTER ONE? ALREADY? NO SECURITY CLEARANCE?** We're just letting YOU, the reader, jump right into `THE SECRET FILES OF THE HOCKEY SUPER SIX?`

We know. You were expecting some sort of security clearance thingamabob before we got started.

Ha! Jokes on you!

We **DID** have a security thingy: The cover of this book!

It's made of the most advanced DNA/RNA and GPA-testing technology, **SO WE ALREADY KNOW EVERYTHING ABOUT YOU**, including that you already know the back story of the Hockey Super Six.

So there's no need to even remind you that they were SIX HOCKEY-LOVING GEEKS . . .

IN OUR PREVIOUS ADVENTURE

SIX HOCKEY-LOVING GEEKS WERE...

WHO ARE YOU CALLING A GEEK?

YEAH... THEY'RE GEEKS.

...ZAPPED BY A MYSTERIOUS FREEZE RAY...

...FIRED BY THIS DUDE, CLARENCE CROSSCHECK.

I'M THE BADDEST GUY!

WITH THE EVILIEST IDEAS!

See how we didn't have to tell you all that old stuff **YOU ALREADY KNOW?**

Will they win this time? Our DNA sensors suggest you believe the answer is **YES**. But we also know that you are a die-hard fan of the (NAME REDACTED) hockey team.

Which also means that you're probably used to bitter disappointment.

Hey, let's catch up with the Super Six, sitting in their Super Six locker room . . .

COULD IT BE TRUE? Are the kids victims of their own success? Are the hockey-playing no-good-doers of the world too scared to challenge the Hockey Super Six?

Let's use the GUMPP security camera network to check in on some of the least-good no-good-doers out there.

Good, good. **CLARENCE CROSSCHECK IS STILL BEHIND BARS.** He seems to be scratching something on the walls of his super-secure cell . . . Maybe a poem? But we're sure it's nothing dangerous.

THE ROBOTS? They're now good — **BUSY DELIVERING PIZZAS** around the globe, on the lookout for plots to destroy the world.

And **MR. FUZZY**, the rabbit? He appears to be doing some **HARMLESS GARDENING** on his family's remote island. Not sure what

crop grows so close to the saltwater of the Pacific Ocean . . . maybe some kind of giant lettuce? That must be why the rabbits are digging so deep.

So everything is fine. **MAYBE IT'S TIME FOR THE SUPER SIX TO TAKE UP SOME HOBBIES?**

NO WAY!

"Non-hockey hobbies?" Wait? Did you feel that? A rumble in the ground? Why is the room shaking? **OH NOOooOOoooO!**

(FOR EVEN MORE SUPER-DISASTROUS EFFECTS -- SHAKE THE BOOK!)

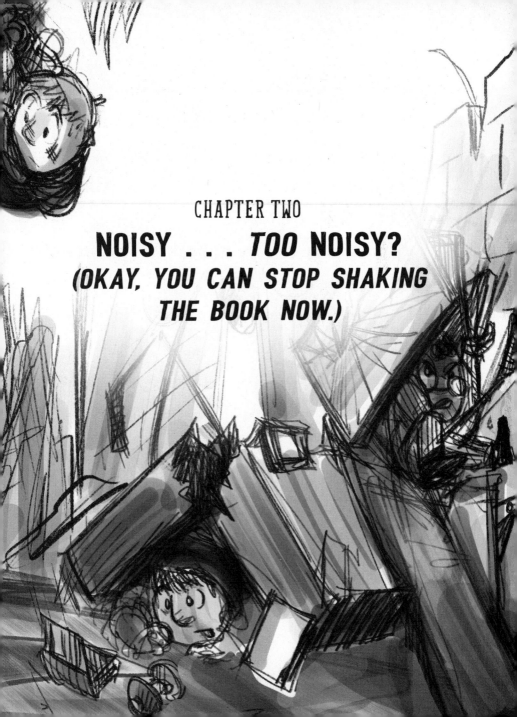

CHAPTER TWO

NOISY . . . *TOO* NOISY?
(OKAY, YOU CAN STOP SHAKING THE BOOK NOW.)

The tremor calmed.

"**WHAT THE HECK WAS THAT?**" asked the twins.

"It felt like an earthquake!" Karl said.

"I knew this was coming," DJ said. "**THE GIANT WORMS ARE TUNNELLING.**"

"Let me guess," the twins said. "The result of underground nuclear tests?"

DJ nodded. "Very slimy and huge. They call them **GOB-ZILLAS.**"

"Goalies," Karl said, rolling his eyes. "That was clearly an earthquake."

"Yeah. Whatever you say, Captain," DJ said with a wink.

"**THE EARTHQUAKE HYPOTHESIS DOES SEEM MORE LIKELY, DJ,**" Starlight said.

"They occur naturally across Canada, and are quite frequent here, although they are not normally felt at this magnitude. Let me show you—"

Starlight was about to explain plate tectonics and the Mattawa and Petawawa Faults,* when Ron Dell, robot pal of the Super Six, leaped through the doorway.

"**URGENT MISSIVE** from Prime Minister Pauline Patinage," Ron said.

"Uh-oh," said the twins, still dangling from the chandelier. "**THAT'S NEVER GOOD.**"

Ron stood still, pressed his butt, and a bright light shone from his eye. The glittering image of Canada's Prime Minister, and Karl's mom, Pauline Patinage, hovered in the air.

---

* So, you'll have to look those up on your own. Okay fine, lazy-head, we'll add an appendix of facts at the end of this book. See Appendix A.

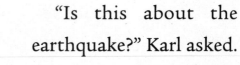

"Is this about the earthquake?" Karl asked.

"Yes. But worse," PM PP said. She took a deep breath. **"SUPER SIX, I'M AFRAID EARTH IS ABOUT TO BE BLOWN TO SMITHEREENS."**

CHAPTER THREE
NOT MY FAULT!

I repeat: **SMITHEREENS**," PM PP said.

"Smithereens is not an actual size category," Starlight said.

"**HOW ABOUT PULVERIZED BACK INTO SUBATOMIC PARTICLES?**"

"Much more clear," Starlight said with a **GULP**.

"It will happen in just a few days," PM Patinage said.

"**NOT IF WE CAN HELP IT.**"

Mo cracked his knuckles. "Um, can we help it?"

"It appears there is no time," PM PP said.

"**WHY? WHAT HAPPENED?**" asked the twins.

"This." PM PP's face was replaced by a satellite image of Mount Logan.

"The **TALLEST MOUNTAIN** in Canada!" Starlight gasped. "**5,959 METRES! AND STILL GROWING!**" Starlight was about to explain why

Mount Logan is indeed still rising* when the image changed suddenly.

A giant beam of **LIGHT BLASTED FROM THE PEAK**, splitting the clouds, ripping the sky, and disappearing into the stars, just narrowly missing the Moon.

"This mysterious ray was fired into space. Observers at the `GUMPP` Moon base—"

"**I KNEW IT!**" DJ said. "GUMPP does have a base on the Moon!"

"Never mind that," PMPatinage added quickly. "The ray was so powerful that it shook the entire planet."

"That's what caused the earthquake we felt?" asked the Six.

----

* Yes, you could look up the reason yourself, but fine . . . we'll add it to the appendix too. See Appendix B.

"Yes. **THAT, AND THE EXPLOSION** when the ray gun itself exploded, leaving only tiny fragments remaining."

"Smithereen sized?" DJ said, nudging Starlight with his elbow.

"Smart evil people," said the twins, "**DON'T LEAVE BEHIND ANY EVIDENCE.**"

"Indeed," said the PM. "Although I have a crack team of experts looking for clues."

"**WAIT. HOW IS THIS RAY GOING TO BLOW UP EARTH IF IT WAS AIMED AT SPACE?**" DJ asked.

A map of the solar system replaced the image of the mountain.

"The ray is, in fact, a **TRACTOR BEAM**," PM Patinage said.

"Someone wants to farm in space?" asked Benny.

"Not that kind of tractor, doofus," Jenny said.

"Jenny is right," Karl said, peering at the map of

the solar system. "This beam looks like it's grabbed a hold of something."

"Using a super-powered gravitational force," Starlight added.

"Exactly," said PM Patinage. **"AND THE OBJECT IT'S PULLING IS A GIANT CHUNK OF ICE."**

"Ice?"

PM PP nodded. "And rock. An asteroid named **HIELO-23B**. Ron, can you zoom in please?"

Ron adjusted his butt and the display showed the grainy image of what looked like a chunk of rock in orbit somewhere in space, being grabbed by an invisible hand and then turning and heading straight for Earth.

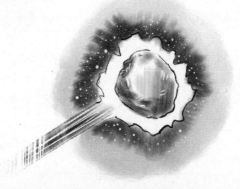

"Looks like a pizza," Mo said.

"You think everything looks like a pizza," DJ said.

PM Patinage sighed. **"IMPACT IS ZERO MINUS THREE DAYS."**

"Who would do such a thing?" asked the twins.

"You may remember that we at **GUMPP** suspected that **CLARENCE CROSSCHECK WAS WORKING WITH OTHER EVIL PEOPLE**," PM Patinage said.* "And we were right. A few seconds after the blast, we received a message from a group called CPPMUG."

All eyes turned to DJ, the resident expert on all weird stuff that you find on the internet and other places.

---

* Readers of *On Thin Ice* will remember PM PP saying this. We'll give you a few seconds to flip back in case you don't believe us . . . TOLD YOU.

"CPPMUG STANDS FOR CRIMINAL PEOPLE PURSUING MALEVOLENT UBER-EVIL GOALS. THE C ISN'T SILENT."

"What did the message say?" Karl asked.

"It said that they will fire a ray from an undisclosed location to destroy the asteroid. BUT only if the governments of the world **SEND ALL OUR GOLD RESERVES** to an untraceable bank account."

"Is that all?" scoffed Benny and Jenny. "Money?"

"AND . . . THEY DEMAND THE DESTRUCTION OF ALL THE WORLD'S HOCKEY RINKS."

"MONSTERS!" said the twins.

MONSTERS!

"I don't know what else we can do," PM PP said. "There's no time left to create our own death ray.

I mean, we're close, but it's not ready yet."

"Sorry, what?" DJ asked.

PM Patinage gave a nervous  cough. "Um. Forget that last bit. The **BOTTOM LINE IS THAT WE'LL HAVE TO GIVE IN TO THEIR DEMANDS.** We've already mobilized hundreds of bulldozers to begin razing the rinks."

"**NOooOoO!**" Benny and Jenny wailed.

"I'm sorry, but we're between a rock and a hard place."

His mother's words tweaked something in Karl's memory. "Or maybe we're between a Rocket and a hard place?"

"Rocket? That joke isn't even funny," DJ said.

Karl ignored him. "**I BELIEVE I SAW A REPORT THAT THE CANADIAN SPACE AGENCY IS ABOUT**

TO LAUNCH A SATELLITE?"

PM Patinage frowned. "You mean that **SECRET REPORT** that was on my desk last night?"

Karl blushed. "Um. Yes."

"Yes. It is true. We're just about to fire a rocket that is designed to expand HD broadcasts of hockey games. Why?"

Karl rubbed his hands together. "**HOCKEY SUPER SIX . . . I'VE GOT AN IDEA.**"

CHAPTER FOUR
BETWEEN A ROCKET AND A HARD PLACE

A few hours later, the Super Six were crammed into an elevator, rising up, up, up beside a sleek blue rocket.

"This idea makes no sense," the twins grumbled.

"On the contrary," Karl said. "The asteroid that CPPMUG has summoned is a solid block of ice."

"Like your head," DJ chuckled.

Karl frowned but continued. **"WHO CONTROLS ICE BETTER THAN ANYONE ELSE, EVER?"**

The twins looked at each other and shrugged. Mo and DJ did the same.

"**WE DO!**" Karl said. He blasted a few snowflakes at his teammates.

OH. YEAH.

Starlight jumped in. "So as our captain has grasped, it stands to reason that if we can get close to this object, we might be able, **USING OUR STRENGTH . . .**"

Mo flexed.

"**INTELLIGENCE . . .**"

Starlight smiled.

"LEADERSHIP . . ."

Karl smiled.

"TEAMWORK . . ."

The twins high-fived.

"And . . ." Starlight looked at DJ for a few seconds. "And . . ."

"Yes?" DJ narrowed his eyes.

"AND . . . OUR ABILITY TO THINK OUTSIDE THE BOX!"

"Nice save," DJ grinned. "And I know all about nice saves."

"ALL of our skills will allow us to divert, destroy or find some other creative solution to this dilemma without sacrificing all the global bank accounts. Or losing our hockey rinks."

"WE MUST STOP THESE MONSTERS!" said the twins.

Starlight shook her head sadly. "Two hundred

have already been destroyed."

"WHO COULD HATE HOCKEY THAT MUCH?" asked Jenny.

"AND WHY?" asked Benny.

The elevator reached the top. Ron was waiting for them, dressed in a safety vest and holding a clipboard. **"WELCOME TO THE RICHARD ROCKET,"** he said.

"She's beautiful!" Starlight said.

"Why, thank you," came a suave voice. "And the ride is incredibly smooth."

They all turned and saw a man in an astronaut suit standing in the doorway. His hair was slicked back in a wave, and as he grinned his teeth seemed to sparkle.

"Allow me to introduce myself."

"No need!" Starlight gasped. **"YOU'RE PYLON RICHARD! THE FAMOUS ASTRO-ENGINEER."**

"Yes. **OF COURSE** you've heard of me," the man laughed. "I sometimes let humility get in the way and **FORGET HOW FAMOUS AND ADORED I AM.**"

The twins exchanged a glance. "Humility?"

"But it is true. I am very famous and incredibly intelligent. **IT WAS MY BRILLIANT IDEA TO GO ON THIS DANGEROUS BUT HEROIC JOURNEY.**"

"BUT, I—" Karl started, but Richard kept going.

"I'm glad your mother listened to me, Craig."

"Karl. But—" Karl tried again.

"She knows a genius when she meets one, I guess." He tapped his brain. "That's why the Canadian government is **PAYING ME GAZILLIONS.**"

"Gazillions is not a real—" Karl began.

Richard barrelled ahead. "And my brilliant plan will work. To make absolutely sure, I will act as captain for our journey."

"But Ron is a pilot and—" began the twins, but Richard ignored them as well.

"Now, enough of all your childish chatter. No more talk. Time is of the essence. Ron, before you go, **HELP THESE CHILDREN GET READY**. Pylon Richard has a few challenging tasks in the cargo bay that only I can perform." Richard strutted through the open cockpit door and deeper inside the rocket.

"Sorry I kept prattling on there," Karl groaned as the Six made their way inside.

"Yeah, Cap'," Mo said. "**I COULD BARELY HEAR RICHARD TELL US ABOUT HOW GREAT RICHARD IS.**"

"I never trust anyone who refers to themselves in the third person," Jenny said.

"Benny agrees," said Benny. Jenny gave him a slug on the shoulder.

"**BUT HE IS A GENIUS!**" Starlight said. "**JUST LOOK AROUND YOU.**"

The cockpit was sleek and stylish, like a luxury car.

"These seats are super comfortable," Benny said, bouncing up and down on the soft fabric. The buttons and lights lit up the whole scene like a movie set.

"Fair enough," DJ said. He leaned on the dashboard and accidentally pushed a switch to ON. The rocket began to roar and shake.

Richard's voice boomed from a hidden speaker. **"DON'T TOUCH ANYTHING, YOU FOOLS!"**

"**OOPS**," DJ said. He flicked the switch back off.

"I guess none of us are actual rocket scientists," the twins admitted.

"Richard has made a beautiful craft. Let's hope it works as well as it looks," Ron said. He took the children to their seats and helped them strap in. "I'll be monitoring the mission from down here, along with the PM."

"Thanks, Ron," said the Six.

Ron smiled. "Good luck."

He closed the door behind him. **A FEW MOMENTS LATER, THE ROCKET BEGAN TO SHAKE.**

"Wasn't me," DJ said.

Ron's voice came over the speakers: **"LIFTOFF IN TEN, NINE . . ."**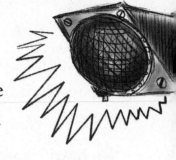

"Where's our fearless pilot?" Mo asked.

PM Patinage's voice joined Ron's: "Super Six, I know how dangerous this mission is . . ."

"SEVEN, SIX . . ."

". . . But I can think of no other team I'd rather have entrusted with saving Earth."

"FOUR, THREE . . ."

"Thanks, Mom!" Karl said.

PM Patinage sniffed. "Come back safely."

"ZERO!"

Richard came zooming back to the cockpit and leaped into his seat.

"LIFTOFF!" he yelled, then laughed long and loud, **A WILD LOOK ON HIS FACE**.

The rocket began to pull away from Earth's gravity, rising steadily into space.

"This IS a smooth ride!" said the twins.

"Of course it is," said Richard. He sounded annoyed. **"ENJOY IT LIKE IT'S YOUR FIRST, AND POSSIBLY LAST, FLIGHT INTO SPACE!"**

Starlight turned to Karl. "Only a true scientific genius could design something so wonderful."

Karl was about to mention that the only other scientific genius he knew had tried to turn a bunny into a super-soldier, but was **AWED INTO SILENCE BY STARS.**

CHAPTER FIVE
YOU CAN'T BE SIRIUS!

As they burst through the last layers of Earth's atmosphere, the window filled with glowing points of light.

"My goodness," said Karl. "Stars!"

"Yes," said Richard. "That bright one is the North Star. If we follow the second to the right of it, we'll arrive at HIELO-23B in a few hours."

He unclasped his seatbelt and began floating in the air. **"AND WE ARE NOW FREE OF EARTH'S GRAVITY."**

"**WELL. MOSTLY FREE,**" said Starlight. "It's more **MICRO-GRAVITY AT THIS POINT.** Faint but there, until we move farther away toward the asteroid."

"Of course I knew that. **I WAS . . . TESTING YOU,**" Richard said.

"**UH-HUH,**" said the twins, exchanging a glance.

"To know so much about space," Richard said, pointing a finger at Starlight. "You must have watched all my videos."

"Well, actually, I studied—" Starlight started.

"That would explain your **APPEARANCE** of heightened intelligence."

"Appearance?"

"**MY INTELLIGENCE DOES RUB OFF ON PEOPLE WHO HEAR ME SPEAK.**" Richard chuckled and patted himself on the back.

"His intelligence sounds like the flu," DJ whispered to the twins.

"ARE YOU AS GOOD AT HOCKEY AS YOU ARE AT SCIENCE?" Karl asked, desperately trying to change the subject.

Richard's smile faltered for just a second, and he gave a very slight shudder. "**I, OF COURSE, LOVE THE GAME.** I mean, who wouldn't?"

He shivered again, then his beaming smile reappeared. "But **MY EXCEPTIONAL INTELLIGENCE**, of course, didn't leave time for **PLAY.**"  He seemed to struggle to say the last word.

"To put that in terms simple enough for you to understand, I chose brains over brawn." He turned to Mo. **"UNLIKE SOME OF YOU."**

Mo looked slightly hurt.

"You can have bo—" Starlight began again.

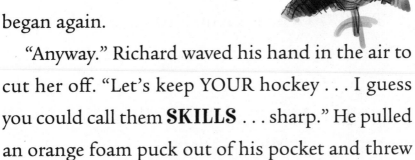

"Anyway." Richard waved his hand in the air to cut her off. "Let's keep YOUR hockey . . . I guess you could call them **SKILLS** . . . sharp." He pulled an orange foam puck out of his pocket and threw it in the air. **"TIME FOR A LITTLE . . . FUN?"**

"It's like **HE DOESN'T KNOW WHAT THAT IS**," DJ whispered to Starlight.

At the mere sight of a puck, the twins undid their belts. In a flash, Benny scooped the puck with his stick. "Here!" Jenny called and took a perfect pass right on the tape and slapped it toward the doorway of the cockpit.

She raised her hand to celebrate. **"THE FIRST GOAL SCORED IN OUTER SPACE!"**

EXCEPT DJ had also undone his belt and leaped in front of the door before the shot could go through. He waved his glove in the air, revealing the puck. **"YOU MEAN THE FIRST GLOVE SAVE IN THE HISTORY OF SPACE!"**

"Both inaccurate," said Starlight. "Russian cosmonauts have played hockey in space before."*

"STOP THE BRAINY BLAH-BLAH-BLAH," said the twins. "LET'S PLAY!"

"EXACTLY. TURN OFF YOUR BRAINS," Richard muttered. He saw that Karl had heard the comment, then smiled his best smile at him. "I meant, don't think about the mission for a few moments. Relax."

----

* See Appendix C if you don't believe us!

"Oh," Karl said. "**I GUESS THAT MAKES SENSE.**"

He wanted to ask Richard a few questions about where they were heading, **SINCE HE WAS SO SMART AND ALL**, but the scientist floated away, fiddling with some dials on the dashboard. And there was a spacey shinny game on. **KARL TEAMED UP WITH MO, AND STARLIGHT JOINED THE TWINS.**

Mo and Karl spent most of their time chasing Jenny and Benny. Finally, DJ made a leg save and kicked the puck straight to Mo, who turned to shoot and realized there was nothing to shoot AT.

"**HEY, MR. RICHARD,**" he said. "We seem to be short one goalie. **YOU WANNA PLAY?**"

Richard definitely sneered. "There is some **INVALUABLE INTELLECTUAL** work I must see to."

"It's the **BRAINIEST** position." DJ waved.

Richard snorted. **"A BRAINLESS ROCK COULD PLAY IT."**

"DJ proves that," said the twins, giving each other high-fives.

"Aw, let him go," DJ said. **"NOT EVERYONE IS SMART ENOUGH TO BE A GOALIE."**

Richard flinched. "Are you questioning my intelli—"

"Yes." DJ tapped his own head. "Maybe I'm smarter than you?"

RICHARD TWITCHED.

"Oh, c'mon," Karl said. "We'll only take soft shots."

"Do you take other kinds?" howled the twins.

Richard now clenched his teeth and trembled, apparently wrestling in some kind of internal debate. It was hard to hear over the twins laughing, but he seemed to be talking to himself. "**SPORTS ARE NOT FOR YOU, PYLON.** You are better than that." Then, "Stay inside and study, Pylon. **STUDY.**"

DJ kept tapping his helmet.

"STOP THAT!" Richard yelled. He stopped shaking. "I will play, but only for two goals."

"You'll be here for a while then," DJ said, waving his pads like he was dancing. "Cause I'm not giving up any."

"Two goals each side," said the twins.

Mo set Richard in front of the control panel. **"IT'LL BE FUN."**

"I doubt that," the scientist mumbled. But he stayed in place.

KARL AND MO SCORED ON THEIR FIRST SHOT EASILY. "I was calculating the angle and speed," Richard said. "But then one of you deflected the puck."

"Uh-huh," Karl replied.

THE NEXT SHOT ALSO WENT IN. "I was screened," Richard said.

Mo and Karl rolled their eyes. It almost looked like Richard wanted to lose the game. But the twins, with Starlight's help, were able to barrage DJ with shots, and the score was soon tied 2–2.

"Game over," Richard said. "That was the deal."

"**NO TIES IN SPACE!**" said the twins.

"Next goal wins," said Starlight.

Starlight took the puck and slid it to Benny. He flipped over top of Mo and then passed the puck through Karl's legs to Jenny. **SHE BLASTED A SHOT THAT WAS LABELLED FOR THE TOP OF THE DOOR.** DJ knew right away that he was too far away to make the save. But then he had an idea. Starlight had told him about **"PROPULSION."**

So he swung his glove up, and at that moment **HE EXPELLED A BURST OF GAS FROM HIS BACK END** that helped propel him in the opposite direction. The action and subsequent reaction gave him just the fraction of a millimetre he needed to tip the puck away from the goal.

"**DISGUSTING,**" Karl said.

"**HE WHO DEALT IT, SAVED IT,**" DJ said, passing the puck to Mo.

Mo turned to slide a **SHOT STRAIGHT AT RICHARD.** "Shoot," Mo said. "**TOO** soft."

Richard ducked, and **THE PUCK FLEW PAST HIM AND DINGED OFF THE CONSOLE.**

"I was screened AND the puck was deflected again!" Richard said with a sniff.

"What? No way!" said the twins.

"**WHAT A CHICKEN,**" DJ whispered to Starlight. "And you know how little I trust chickens."

"We won!" Mo and Karl began screeching and hollering.

Ron's voice came over the speakers. "Listen to them, PM PP! **THEY'RE DYING!**

Curse my rubber body, *I KNEW THIS TRIP WAS A BAD IDEA.*"

Karl floated over. "No, Ron. We're all right. We're all right!"

"Whew!" Ron said. *"WELL, YOU NEED TO GET READY FOR LANDING."*

"WE TRAVELLED THAT FAST?" Starlight seemed shocked.

Ron continued. "I'm afraid HIELO-23B is increasing in speed. You need to intercept immediately."

Richard waved toward the seats. **"HURRY, CHILDREN. IT IS ALMOST TIME TO END THIS, FOREVER."**

"What an odd choice of words," Karl thought.

CHAPTER SIX

A COMPUTER CHIP OFF THE OLD BLOCK

Anne Droid and Rob Ott stood on the top of Mount Logan holding hands.

The remains of the giant laser cannon was spread out in a debris field all around them, like flecks of pepper in the salt-white snow.

"NOT SURE THERE IS A LOT OF USEFUL EVIDENCE LEFT HERE," Ott said. He reluctantly let go of Anne's hand and began walking around, carefully avoiding the shards of twisted metal.

"Maybe a microscopic scan look will **REVEAL**

SOMETHING," Anne said. She knelt down and began probing for any clues about who had made and fired the tractor beam.

She smiled as she spied Ott doing the same thing. Their lives had changed so much over the last few months. Anne was embarrassed to think how close they had come to **HELPING THE TWISTED CLARENCE CROSSCHECK** take over the Canadian government. Now their new friend, Prime Minister Pauline Patinage, had asked them to take a break from global espionage — disguised as pizza deliverers — to climb an inhospitable mountain.

The wind whipped. Snow and bitter gusts made the mountaintop dangerous, for humans anyway. But Anne and Rob were happy to be doing it together. Besides, robots **DON'T FEEL THE COLD**.

"Something seems familiar about these wiring junctions," Ott said. He held an almost microscopic fragment of a computer chip to his right eye. **HE ACTIVATED HIS X-RAY VISION.** Anne could simultaneously see what he was looking at in her own electronic brain.

"OH NO!" She gasped. **"WE NEED TO WARN THE PM RIGHT AWAY!"**

CHAPTER SEVEN
MILKY WAYLAID

The view of the asteroid began to fill the window. It had started to glow faintly around the edges as it drew closer to the light and heat of the sun.

"**IT REALLY DOES LOOK LIKE A HUGE HOCKEY RINK,**" said the twins.

"Are those lines painted on the surface?" Starlight said. "**BUT THAT'S IMPOSSIBLE!**"

Richard gave a quick cough, pulled back on the controls, and the asteroid disappeared from view. "**TIME TO LAND.**"

DJ whispered to Mo. "I hope he's a better pilot than goalie."

Mo chuckled. "So, Captain and Starlight, **ANY IDEA WHAT WE DO WHEN WE LAND?**"

Richard fired the blasters to lower the ship and it began to fall slowly in reverse. **HE ALSO LEANED IN CLOSER TO THE KIDS.**

"A few. For example . . ." Karl spotted Richard craning an ear.

He lowered his voice. "Maybe we skate at high speed in one direction." He definitely saw Richard raise an eyebrow.

"It's also possible," Starlight added, "that we could use the force of our shots, or super-skating, to crack the asteroid into pieces."

DID RICHARD SNORT?

"What if the tractor beam is still active?" Mo asked.

"Perhaps we can deflect it," Starlight said, tapping her lip.

"Deflecting is our specialty," said the twins.

"It's certainly not back-checking," DJ said.

Benny hurled the orange puck at DJ, who blockered it away. "Or shooting," he grinned.

Richard was almost falling out of his chair **TRYING TO HEAR THE CONVERSATION.**

Karl decided it was maybe time to **STOP** talking. "Well, let's wait and see what the surface is like before we make any final decisions." **THEN HE HELD A FINGER TO HIS LIPS.**

Starlight cocked her head, but saw the look in Karl's eyes and nodded.

"YOU'RE ALL AWFULLY QUIET ALL OF A SUDDEN," Richard said.

"Just **MARVELLING** at your expert piloting," Karl said.

Richard beamed and settled back in his seat. "Well, of course you are. **WHO WOULDN'T BE!?!** It takes incredible concentration and mental flexibility to excel at this task."

DJ GROANED.

"Are the lowered oxygen levels causing you to groan?" Richard asked.

"Not exactly," DJ said.

"Well, we're about to land, so grab one of my space helmets from under your seats."

"No need. We've got our own built in." Starlight pushed a button and her visor expanded, enclosing her head in super-hard plastic. The others did the same.

"Very clever," Richard said quietly. "But we'll see **HOW** clever in just a few moments."

There was a gentle thump as the ship touched down on the **SURFACE OF HIELO-23B**.

CHAPTER EIGHT
STILL MORE TO COMET

Ron and PM Patinage huddled at her desk, watching **RICHARD'S LIVE STREAM** of the Super Six's mission to save Earth.

The asteroid appeared as a fuzzy smudge on their screen, then disappeared as Richard banked the shuttle up to land.

"Everything seems good so far," Ron said.

"I'm still not sure why everyone made those **WEIRD FACES** when DJ made that last save," PM Patinage said.

Ron shrugged. "Oh, look! They are about to land!"

A puff of ice crystals rose as the thrusters activated and allowed the capsule to land, momentarily blocking the view. Then the camera angle changed to show the frozen surface of the asteroid.

PM Patinage pressed her nose against the screen. **"WHAT ARE THOSE HUGE THINGS IN THE DISTANCE?"**

"I'll begin scanning the feed to get a higher resolution," Ron said.

But before he could do that, two things happened.

First, Mr. Filbert, PM Patinage's assistant, sprinted into the room holding a computer printout. "You need to see this **IMMEDIATELY!**"

The paper showed a super-blown-up image of a **SLIVER OF A COMPUTER CHIP**. A series of etched letters were barely visible on the scoured surface.

A fragment of a name. But enough.

Then the second thing happened. There was a squawk from the computer screen, **AND THE LIVE FEED OF THE MISSION WENT DEAD**.

CHAPTER NINE
GALACTICKED OFF

The side door of the ship opened with a whoosh.

"We have arrived," Richard said. "You heroes go first."

The Six made their way over to the open doorway. Stairs lowered from the ship, touching down on the surface of the killer asteroid.

Now that they were actually there, they could see that HIELO-23B didn't just look like a hockey rink. **IT WAS A HOCKEY RINK.** A net stood at each end. There were faceoff circles, centre and blue lines. The ice was smooth and slick. **A LONE PUCK SAT ON THE CENTRE FACEOFF DOT.**

"**HOW STRANGE,**" Richard said. "I, of course, have **NEVER** been here before, so this is clearly all new to me too!"

Karl's **INNER ALARM BELLS**, already warmed up, **BEGAN TO GO OFF**. He stole a look back at Richard, who was **GRINNING FROM EAR TO EAR**.

Karl had some questions, but Starlight rolled up to him on the platform. "**LOOK HOW EXCITED RICHARD IS TO SEE US SAVE EARTH!**"

"Is that why he's rubbing his hands together and giggling?"

"Why else? And anyway, as Ron observed, the asteroid seems to be **INCREASING IN SPEED**. We don't have much time to debate next steps."

Karl stole one more look back at Richard, who was now bouncing from one foot to the other. But Starlight was right. **TIME WAS RUNNING OUT**, and they were on a **MISSION TO SAVE EARTH**. He'd just have to be even more on his guard.

The twins emerged and, at the sight of the fresh rink, rushed past Karl and scrambled down the steps.

Well, not quite **PAST** Karl. More like **THROUGH** Karl.

Karl tumbled down after them, landing on his back with a **WHUMP**. He pushed himself up, then stared at his hands. **THE ASTEROID FELT . . . WEIRDLY FAMILIAR**. And why wasn't he floating off into space?

"**THE ICE IS AMAZING!**" the twins called. They grabbed the puck and began swooping and skating at super speed.

Starlight joined them on her sledge, rubbing her gloved hand across the ice surface. It was still perfectly smooth despite the energetic cutting of the twin's criss-crossing blades. "**AMAZING. THERE ALSO SEEMS TO BE SOME SORT OF GRAVITY FIELD.**"

Karl rubbed his bruised rear end. "No kidding."

"But what's strange is that the asteroid isn't really large enough to create a gravitational force adequate to keep us tethered to the surface. But what else could be—"

Richard interrupted. "How strange. And this completely impossible force **KEEPS THE PUCK AND NETS FROM FLOATING AWAY. WOW.**"

"And it keeps us from flying away too," DJ said, skating past her and out onto the ice.

"Yes," said Richard, grinning and rubbing his hands together. "But it seems to be a WEAK force, so be careful. A really hard check and, well . . ." he fluttered his hands in the air, ". . . you could end up flying off into the dark, cold void of space. Forever." **HIS GRIN GREW LARGER.**

But the Six did not see that. They were now skating and playing, momentarily forgetting the dire nature of their mission.

"THIS IS INCREDIBLE!" Mo said. He could dig into the ice as hard as possible with his mighty legs and barely scratch the surface. **"IT'S LIKE THE PERFECT RINK!"** he said.

"I wish we'd had ice this good when we'd played those robots!" said the twins.

Karl frowned. They DID have ice this good, once he'd been able to make it himself. "Something about the hardness of this ice seems familiar," he said to Starlight.

"**SPACE IS REALLY COLD**, like around minus 270 degrees Celsius. So maybe it's a **PERFECT ENVIRONMENT** for a hockey rink."

Karl shook his head. "I think it's more than that. I've felt an odd tingling in my fingers and toes ever since we stepped on the asteroid. **I THINK IT'S MADE FROM THE SAME ELEMENT THAT GAVE US OUR POWERS.**"

Starlight gasped. "You mean?"

"**FROZEUM 7.**" Karl nodded. "That might also be what's keeping us tied down. And I think it's no accident that CPPMUG **CHOSE THIS ASTEROID** to threaten Earth. There's more going on than meets the eye."

Before he could explain his suspicions, **THE ASTEROID BEGAN TO SHAKE**.

CHAPTER TEN

THE GRAVITY OF THE SITUATION

The printout floated for a moment then landed on the red carpet of the PM's office. PM Patinage and Ron had rushed away so quickly they'd made an instant breeze. **THE SIX WERE IN SERIOUS DANGER**. Filbert had prepped the fastest GUMPP helicopter, and Ron and the PM had flown off.

A few hours later a cleaner picked up the paper from the floor. "What's I-C-H-A-R-D?" Then she shrugged and tossed the paper into the recycling bin.

CHAPTER ELEVEN
QUAKING IN THEIR SKATES

An earthquake in space?" DJ said, falling on his back and bouncing up and down. The twins, also on the ice, tried to sneak a goal past him, but he snagged it out of the air.

"HA!" he said, waving the puck. "Even an earthquake can't stop me!"

"IT'S NOT AN EARTHQUAKE," Richard said. **"LOOK. LOOK!"**

He jabbed a finger toward the far end of the asteroid. **EMERGING FROM THE SHADOWS WERE**

SIX OF THE STRANGEST CREATURES THE SIX HAD EVER SEEN. Each had eight clawed appendages and a long snout which seemed to be both mouth and nose, with spiked teeth lining the inside. Their eyes were mostly hidden under flaps of folded skin. And each was wearing skates and a holding long wooden hockey stick.

"**ALIEN SASQUATCHES!**" DJ cried.

"No," Starlight said. "I believe these are **TARDIGRADES**."

"Giant, hockey-playing tardigrades?" said the twins.

"I thought tardigrades were **SUPER TINY**," Karl said.

"These must have been **SUPERSIZED**," Starlight said.

"BUT WE DESTROYED THE LAST SIZEMATRON," Mo said.

"Perhaps we were wrong," Starlight said.

"Yes," said Richard. "Perhaps you were **DEAD WRONG**." He cackled. The Six swung around to face him.

The scientist was still standing on the platform above the stairs. Except the stairs were gone, folded back up inside the shuttle. And the shuttle itself was now floating high above the surface of the asteroid.

"RICHARD!" Karl yelled. **"WHAT ARE YOU DOING?"**

"Getting ready to **OBSERVE MY EXPERIMENT.**"

"Experiment?"

"Yes," he said, his smile replaced with a scowl. "An experiment **TO PROVE THAT HOCKEY IS FOR BRUTES, UNWORTHY OF TRUE HUMAN EFFORT.**"

"**YOU CAN HAVE BOTH BRAINS AND BRAWN!**" Starlight said, finally blurting out what she'd tried to tell Richard at least a dozen times since they'd left Earth. "For crying out loud."

"**MY HYPOTHESIS SAYS OTHERWISE.**" Richard laughed and started flipping in circles in the air. "And the battle that's about to begin will prove me right. Even the **IOTA OF USEFUL INTELLIGENCE** you've shown me so far **WILL BE OF NO HELP TO YOU.**"

Richard stopped spinning and sat on the edge of the platform, resting his head on his hands. "It's sometimes hard to keep my scientific objectivity. Alas, a part of me will **ENJOY WATCHING YOU DEFEATED BY BRUTE FORCE.**"

"**WE WON'T PLAY,**" Karl yelled. He threw down his stick and crossed his arms. "We don't have time for this!"

"Au contraire, mon ami," Richard said. "This is ALL you have time for. **IF YOU DON'T PLAY, I DON'T FIRE THE ANTI-TRACTOR BEAM** that sends this asteroid back into space."

"**YOU? YOU?**" Starlight shook with rage. "**YOU'RE CPPMUG?**"

"**JUST** the leader. There are a few other members. That pitiful **CROSSCHECK PROVED TO BE THE WEAKEST.** Do you know why?

HIS LOVE FOR HOCKEY WAS HIS DOWNFALL. It eroded his intelligence."

"If you hate hockey so much," Mo said. "Then why make us play?"

"To prove my point that **HOCKEY IS, AND ALWAYS WAS, A GAME FOR BRUTES.**"

Mo shook his head. "**IT CAN BE. THAT DOESN'T MEAN IT IS.**"

"Or has to be," added the others.

Richard scoffed. "It is and always has been. **THESE HORRIBLE BEASTS ARE THE PERFECT HOCKEY PLAYERS**. And in just seconds they will begin their brutal attack!"

The tardigrades had reached the rink. They clambered over the edge of the icy boards and formed a line at centre ice.

The largest one raised its snout in the air and released a loud, long blast.

The asteroid continued to hurtle toward Earth.

The Six were trapped on top.

DOOM SEEMED CERTAIN.

COULD THINGS GET WORSE?

YES.

The tardigrades began tapping their sticks on the ice, faster and faster, then they rushed at the Six.

"GAME ON!" Richard boomed.

But wait . . . Before the **TARDIGRADE DEATH MATCH** begins, you're probably wondering, how did these hockey-playing giants come to be living on HIELO-23B?

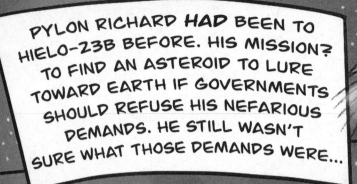

PYLON RICHARD **HAD** BEEN TO HIELO-23B BEFORE. HIS MISSION? TO FIND AN ASTEROID TO LURE TOWARD EARTH IF GOVERNMENTS SHOULD REFUSE HIS NEFARIOUS DEMANDS. HE STILL WASN'T SURE WHAT THOSE DEMANDS WERE...

I JUST NEED TO MAKE THIS ASTEROID A *LITTLE* BIGGER AND IT WILL BE PERFECT!

HE FIRED HIS SIZEMATRON 2001*

LITTLE DID HE SUSPECT THERE WERE MICROSCOPIC TARDIGRADES IN THE LINE OF FIRE.

* A SLIGHT UPGRADE ON THE VERSION HIS *RIVAL EVIL DUDE CLARENCE CROSSCHECK* HAD DESIGNED.

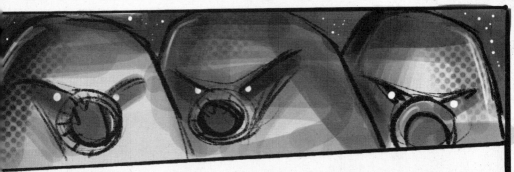

THE ASTEROID GREW, BUT SO DID THE TARDIGRADES. RICHARD WAS SO SHOCKED HE DROPPED THE RAY GUN, WHICH SHATTERED ON THE SUPER-COOLED FROZEUM SURFACE.

THE NOISE STARTLED THE TARDIGRADES, WHO TURNED ON RICHARD. HE RAN BACK TO HIS SPACESHIP, JETTISONED HIS CARGO, AND BEAT A HASTY RETREAT. THE CARGO? HOCKEY EQUIPMENT, STOLEN FROM DONATION BINS -- EQUIPMENT RICHARD WAS GOING TO RELEASE INTO SPACE. ALL PART OF HIS PLAN TO DESTROY HOCKEY.

WHY DID HE HATE HOCKEY SO MUCH?

WAIT? WHAT?!
A BONUS COMIC?

A COMIC **WITHIN** A COMIC?!

Without further ado . . .

THE ORIGIN OF

PYLON RICHARD'S
TWISTED HATRED
OF HOCKEY

5¢
BOY
WHO DIDN'T PLAY
YES! STUDY. STUDY, STUDY!!!
HOW FOOLISH THEY ALL LOOK. MY BRAIN WILL SOMEDAY DEFEAT THEM ALL!

YOUNG PYLON WATCHED OTHER CHILDREN ON WINTER DAYS, ENJOYING THEMSELVES. BUT HIS TUTOR, AGNES BOREHEAD, ALWAYS TOLD HIM HE WAS FAR TOO INTELLIGENT TO JOIN THEM.

"TRUE GREATNESS IS HERE," SHE'D SAY, POINTING AT HER HEAD.

HE'D BEEN DISAPPOINTED, JEALOUS EVEN. BUT HE'D TORN HIS GAZE AWAY AND FOCUSED ON THE NUMBERS AND FORMULAE THAT BROUGHT HIM SO MUCH JOY.

AND AGNES SNEERED AT THE CHILDREN OUTSIDE: "LOOK HOW THEY REVEL IN KNOCKING SOMEONE ELSE DOWN. WHAT A WASTE OF KINETIC ENERGY."

STILL, EVERY DAY BEFORE SITTING DOWN TO HIS CALCULUS, ASTROPHYSICS AND CHEMISTRY, YOUNG PYLON STOLE A LOOK OUT THE WINDOW... UNTIL AGNES NAILED HIS CHAIR TO THE FLOOR SO THAT IT ONLY FACED HIS COMPUTER SCREEN.

AS THE WINTERS PASSED, HIS JEALOUSY TURNED TO SPITE. IF HE COULDN'T PLAY HOCKEY, WHY SHOULD ANYONE ELSE? IT WAS CLEARLY AN ACTIVITY MEANT FOR LESSER PEOPLE.

AGNES SMILED AT EACH INSULT HE NOW ADDED TO HERS.

HE BECAME RICH. HE BECAME SUCCESSFUL. AND HE VOWED THAT ONE DAY HE WOULD DESTROY HOCKEY ITSELF.

STEALING AND DESTROYING DONATED EQUIPMENT WAS JUST ONE PART OF THE PLAN.

BUT IT SOON LED TO HIS EPIPHANY...

AND NOW BACK TO... THE TARDIGRADES' ORIGIN! THE TARDIGRADES RUMMAGED THROUGH THE HOCKEY EQUIPMENT. THEN THEY BEGAN PLAYING, AS IF THEY HAD BEEN BORN TO THE SPORT.

BRAINLESS DOLTS! PERFECT FOR MY MISSION!

AS RICHARD FLEW AWAY FROM HIELO-23B ON THAT FATEFUL DAY, HE BEGAN FORMULATING A PLAN.

AND WHEN HE HEARD CROSSCHECK REPORT THAT SIX CHILDREN HAD BEEN THWARTING THEIR PLANS FOR GLOBAL DOMINATION... THROUGH HOCKEY... ALL THE PARTS OF RICHARD'S PLAN FELL INTO PLACE.

WHAT ARE ALL THE PARTS OF THAT PLAN?

STAY TUNED!

CHAPTER TWELVE
MAKING THE TARDIGRADE

The tardigrades picked up speed.

"If they hit us with adequate force, **WE COULD BE TOSSED INTO SPACE**," Starlight said.

Mo leaped in front of his friends. "I can take the brunt," he said. He dug his skates into the ice.

The others joined him in a line. "We're a team," Karl said, looking up at Mo.

Mo nodded and they all looped arms.

The ice shook with each approaching stride.

Then, just as the tardigrades reached the Six, they stopped. They began **SNIFFING AND SNIFFING** around them.

"See!" Karl called up to Richard. "Hockey doesn't have to be brutish."

"Oh, just wait," Richard said.

The tardigrades **ZEROED IN ON DJ, AND POUNCED**.

"HELP! I'M GETTING CRUSHED!" DJ said, and he disappeared under a pile of sniffing giants.

Richard laughed.

Mo tried to lift off the first tardigrade, but despite his super strength, the beast barely budged. Instead they kept **SNIFFING AND SNUFFLING, AND CRUSHING** the Super Six's goalie.

Karl tried blasting them with ice, but while it slowed them for a millisecond, it didn't stop them.

"DJ!" Starlight said. **"I THINK THEY'RE AFTER THE PUCK!"**

"OK," came a muffled voice.

A black puck spurted out from the pile and flew through the air. The tardigrades watched it rise, then fall on the ice. Moving faster than seemed possible, they leaped off DJ and **CHASED THE PUCK**. They began expertly passing and shooting it between them.

"They are really good," Mo said.

"And heavy," DJ said, gasping for air.

"WE'LL SHOW THEM SOME REAL HOCKEY!" said Benny and Jenny.

The twins bolted out onto the ice, trying to get the puck, but the tardigrades blocked them with their bulk. One, with just a slight twist, **SENT JENNY FLYING THROUGH THE AIR**. Benny had to race to grab her by the hair before she spun out into space.

"SEE!" Richard cackled. "The **MORE BRUTISH YOU ARE, THE BETTER YOU ARE** at this silly game. **EVEN YOU**, with your **MARGINALLY** useful brains, are no match for their unthinking power!"

The largest tardigrade looked up at Richard for a long time.

"What are you staring at, you **BRAINLESS LOUT?**" Richard called down. **"GO PLAY. SCOOT! SHOO!"**

The tardigrade turned to the kids and shook his head.

"If that thing could roll its eyes it would," Karl said.

"INTERESTING," Starlight said.

Karl allowed himself a smile. When Starlight called something "interesting" it usually meant she was working out something in her super brain.

THEN THE TARDIGRADE MOTIONED TO THE RINK.

"ARE THEY ASKING US TO PLAY A GAME?" Karl asked.

"It would appear so," Starlight said. "Perhaps they are not as brainless as Richard thinks?"

A tardigrade took a shot so hard it **SHATTERED THE BLADE** of DJ's high-tech super goalie stick.

"OR MAYBE NOT."

CHAPTER THIRTEEN
AWFUL BLAST OFF

You might think that Ron and PM Patinage were on their way to fly a rocket to save the kids.

You'd be wrong. Well, sort of.

PM Patinage already knew that Richard's was the only **KNOWN** rocket that was capable of reaching HIELO-23B in time. And it was already in space.

But she had had an idea. So they were headed for the last place you'd ever suspect they'd be heading: a maximum security **GUMPP** facility deep in the mountains of British Columbia's Okanagan Valley.

"CLARENCE **CROSSCHECK!**" PM Patinage shouted as the doors to his super-secure cell slid open.

Crosscheck was on the verge of leaping through the hole he'd just burned in the solid titanium wall. He quickly slid a framed poster of himself in front of the hole and kicked over the chair he'd been using as a ladder.

"Redecorating?" asked Ron, narrowing his eye at his former boss. Crosscheck gave a nervous cough and sidled away from the picture.

"Let me guess the reason for this visit," Crosscheck said. "That earthquake I felt had **something to do with PYLON RICHARD**."

PM Patinage looked shocked. "How did you know?"

"Simple. His tractor beam is **one of ONLY three inventions** capable of blasting with such monumental force."

"What are the other two?" asked the PM.

"Other two what?" Crosscheck said, his eyes now darting back and forth.

PM Patinage glared at him. "We'll deal with that later. We're here because, and this will sound bizarre, **WE NEED YOUR HELP**."

Crosscheck's grin spread across his face and he gave a hollow laugh. "And **why would I help you?** To say thanks for my wonderful living arrangements?"

PM Patinage had been thinking about this on the flight over, and had an answer. "No. Because as twisted as you are . . ."

"Thank you."

"... YOU **STILL LOVE** HOCKEY."

Crosscheck's grin vanished. **"He WOULDN'T."**

Ron projected the CPPMUG demands onto the wall. "The main demand from your buddy Pylon is that **WE DESTROY ALL THE WORLD'S HOCKEY RINKS**. Because time is so tight, we've already 'decommissioned' twenty or so."

Crosscheck began to shake. He kept stealing looks at his portrait. If he just said he didn't care, these annoying fools would leave and he'd escape. But escape into what? **A WORLD WITHOUT HOCKEY?**

Then an even more horrible idea occurred to his horrible brain. "Wait. **WHERE** were these rinks you destroyed?"

PM Patinage paused. "The demands specifically dictated that we begin with the **PENTICTON DOUBLE TROUBLE RINKARAMA**."

Crosscheck gasped. Before his disgusting goalie equipment had taken over his soul, he'd been a kid who **DREAMED OF BEING A GREAT PLAYER**. Something about this news woke a dying memory deep within him, of cold pre-dawn mornings with his mum helping him tie his skates . . . on a wooden bench . . . in the Penticton Double Trouble Rinkarama.

A single tear ran down Crosscheck's face. Even he, evil **Clarence Crosscheck**, had a limit on the evil he'd inflict on the world. And Pylon Richard, his colleague and rival, had crossed it.

HE'D ESCAPE LATER.

"Fine. I'll help. But we're going to need a match, hockey tape, chewing gum and a large bag of peanuts."

CHAPTER FOURTEEN
DOWN AND OUTER SPACE

The Six had to admit it, the tardigrades were tough to play. **REALLY TOUGH.** The tardigrade goalie had actually fallen asleep because the twins had only been able to **GET OFF ONE SHOT ON NET**, and it had been from a horrible angle — dinging off the post before skipping harmlessly back to centre ice.

DJ had been able to stave off an onslaught of hard shots, but his equipment was looking ragged. Chunks of his blocker and pads kept breaking off and were now in orbit around the asteroid.

Mo had almost been hip-checked into space **TWICE**. Only quick reflexes from the twins and Starlight, including an improvised human pyramid, had saved him.

Richard was watching the whole thing from his perch on the shuttle platform, laughing and taking notes on a tablet. At one point he held it up and showed the Six video of hockey rinks being blown up and plowed under.

The Six had attempted to quit the game, but Richard said if they didn't play he'd just blast off into space and **LET THE ASTEROID DESTROY EARTH** and, by extension, **EVERY HOCKEY RINK ON EARTH AND ON HIELO-23B**.

"My brilliant plan is unfolding one way or another! Now keep playing."

"TIME OUT!" Karl called.

"You mean time is running out!" Richard called. "Better hurry."

Earth **WAS** growing in size on the horizon.

"He's like some maniacal Roman emperor," Starlight said, jerking her head toward Richard.

"But I thought he was an amazing genius," Karl said with a growl.

"Fine. I was a little overly awed," Starlight groaned. "And he **IS** a genius. But I believe he has made a **FUNDAMENTAL ERROR**. Using only your brains is just as dangerous as brawn alone."

"And your evidence for that?" DJ asked, waving the splintered remains of his goalie stick.

"Yes, the tardigrades are using their size to their advantage," Starlight said. "But they are also clearly **FAR MORE INTELLIGENT** than Richard gives them credit for. He's just biased against anyone who's good at hockey."

Karl nodded. "Just look at the way they played their positions on that last faceoff. They set up a really nice tip to the side of the net before Starlight could get out to the point."

"**THAT WAS A PRETTY SWEET MOVE**," Jenny had to admit.

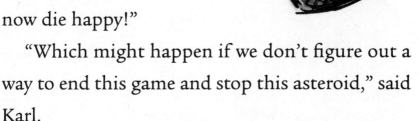

"**AND A NICE SAVE**," Benny said.

DJ flinched. "Complimented by the twins? I can now die happy!"

"Which might happen if we don't figure out a way to end this game and stop this asteroid," said Karl.

Mo shook his head. "**WHAT THE HECK IS RICHARD HOPING TO ACHIEVE WITH THIS GAME?**"

Starlight looked out at the tardigrades, who were slipping the puck back and forth. "He is a scientist, even if he's an evil one, and **HE IS TESTING A HYPOTHESIS.**"

"Which is?"

"That **HOCKEY IS BAD** because it, in his view, doesn't require thought, brains, intelligence. If we lose, it justifies his decision to hate, and therefore destroy, hockey."

"So what happens if we win?"

Starlight had no answer for that. "It's possible that he will, as a scientist, reconsider his hypothesis."

Mo looked up at the gleeful Richard. "So far that does not seem likely."

"Neither does winning," said Karl.

"GAME BACK ON!" Richard called. "Next goal, which seems likely to be the only goal, wins."

"Let's show that blowhard that **WE CAN WIN THIS THING**," said the Six. They laid their hands together and raised them in the air with a cheer.

But it proved just as difficult as before.

More and more of DJ's equipment joined the growing ring of debris. The tardigrades **FORMED A WALL** in front of their goalie, **BLOCKING SHOT AFTER SHOT**. Mo bounced off them again and again trying to squeeze by. The twins tried flipping the puck. **THEY TRIED SHOOTING LOW, HIGH. NOTHING** GOT THROUGH.

"**WHAT DO WE DO?**" DJ yelled, watching another fragment of blocker spinning away. "The next shot is going to hit bone."

Karl and Starlight huddled together as the twins saved Mo from flying away one more time. Then they turned to face their beleaguered keeper.

"**DJ, WE HAVE A PLAN. AND YOU'RE GOING TO HATE IT.**"

CHAPTER FIFTEEN
ORBIT BY BIT

PM Patinage wasn't sure what she'd expected Clarence Crosscheck to do to help them, but she'd been desperate.

Now they were **ALL SITTING INSIDE** what appeared to be a **LARGE GARBAGE CAN**, inside a grain silo, outside the city of Weyburn, Saskatchewan.

The gum, PM Patinage was shocked to discover, was to **SEAL A LEAK IN THE GLASS WINDSHIELD** of what Crosscheck called his **"prototype projectile."** She didn't want to ask what the tape and peanuts were for.

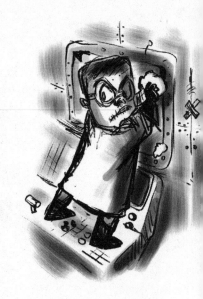

"Not exactly as sleek as a Richard Rocket," PM Patinage observed.

Crosscheck hovered his finger over a large red button that read **EJECT**. "Would you like to leave?"

PM Patinage made a mental note to tone down her criticism. But she was still nervous. "Why 'projectile' and not 'rocket ship'?" she asked.

Crosscheck fiddled with a few loose dials and wires. He pounded the ceiling and the lights flickered on.

"It's NOT, technically, designed to carry humans, or robots," he nodded at Ron.

Ron gulped. He'd seen that ruthless look in Crosscheck's eye many times. "This is the lunar missile you were always talking about, isn't it?"

Crosscheck glared at his former assistant. "Yes. The one we would have finished if you hadn't **abandoned** me."

PM Patinage slapped her forehead. "Are you saying this **TIN CAN ISN'T FINISHED?**"

"The ejector seat is," Crosscheck said, hovering his finger over the button.

"I mean tin can in the nicest way," PM Patinage said.

Crosscheck took more chewed gum out of his

mouth and stuck it on the gap between the glass and the metal hull.

"That should do it."

Ron and PM Patinage exchanged nervous glances. Before they had time to rethink this adventure, Crosscheck struck a match, lit the bag of peanuts, and threw it over his shoulder.

There was an explosion as it hit some kind of gas, and **THE PROJECTILE LURCHED UPWARD INTO SPACE.**

"Now it's a fifty-fifty chance," Crosscheck said, sitting back in his chair.

"Between success and failure?" asked Ron.

"No. Between **reaching HIELO-23B OR crashing into the Arctic Ocean with a boom.**"

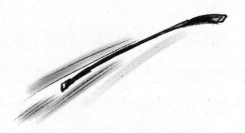

CHAPTER SIXTEEN
STAR CHECK

Not in a gazillion years," DJ said.

"We don't have a gazillion years," Karl said. "Who knows **HOW** much time we have?"

"But I almost got **CRUSHED** last time! AND my equipment was at least a metre thicker!"

Starlight slapped DJ's pad with her stick.

"OUCH!" he said.

"Sorry. Look. It's our last chance."

DJ gazed out at the twins. They'd managed to steal the puck from the tardigrades, but were

UNABLE TO BREAK THROUGH THE WALL to get a decent shot on net. Richard continued to laugh and dance. Earth was now **THE SIZE OF A DIME**.

DJ let out a loud sigh. "Fine. But you better make it fast. Like my glove hand."

Starlight nodded. Then she called to Benny and Jenny, who were skating so much they were actually getting tired. Mo kept trying to push through the wall of tardigrades, but continued to bounce backward.

"JENNY AND BENNY: OPERATION OOPS-A-DIZZY."

Jenny stopped. She looked down at the puck, confused. **"REALLY?"**

"YES!" Karl yelled.

Jenny shook her head sadly, then slid a perfect

pass to **BENNY, WHO WAS RACING . . . TOWARD HIS OWN NET**.

"What are you doing?" Richard howled.

Benny wound up.

"Nice and easy, you meathead," DJ mumbled.

But Benny just couldn't fight his instincts and he gunned a shot labelled for the top corner. DJ's hand shot out at lightning speed. He howled as the puck disintegrated the remains of the webbing, bent his fingers, and then fell to the ice. **IT EDGED TOWARD THE GOAL LINE.**

DJ leaned back, but his broken stick couldn't reach and he toppled over.

SLOWLY, SLOWLY, THE PUCK TRICKLED TOWARD THE GOAL.

The tardigrades **CHARGED.**

Victory now seemed assured.

Starlight began furiously stabbing at the ice with her sticks, moving faster and faster and faster.

Just as the puck was about to cross the line, she shot out the front of her sledge and tipped it just the slightest fraction of a whisker. **IT WORKED!** The puck came to a **REST AGAINST THE POST** as Starlight flew past the goal and crashed into the far boards.

DJ found his feet and **JUMPED ON THE PUCK** before the tardigrades could tap it into the goal.

Then, instead of sliding it back out for a faceoff, he stayed lying on top. "Hurry, hurry, hurry," he muttered.

The tardigrades exchanged confused looks, approaching DJ slowly, sniffing and snurfling like they had before.

DJ rolled onto his back, clutching the puck tightly to his chest. The largest tardigrade jumped, then so did the others. DJ let out a grunt as **THE FULL WEIGHT OF THE BEASTS LANDED ON TOP OF HIM**, trying to wrestle the puck free.

"HAHAHAHAHAHA!" Richard laughed. "Well, this has been fun. But I must be going now."

Karl tore his gaze away from the pile. "What do you mean?"

"Well, my hypothesis has been proven. **HOCKEY DESERVES TO BE DESTROYED.**"

"But it's still **ZERO-ZERO!**" yelled Mo.

Richard shrugged. "You've had ample time to prove me wrong. Now it's time to return to Earth and count my money."

"Whatever," said the twins. "**AND REVEL IN THE DESTRUCTION OF ALL THE WORLD'S HOCKEY RINKS.**"

"**MONSTER!**" yelled the twins. They threw their sticks, which clanged off the side of the shuttle and spun off into the darkness.

"Tsk-tsk," Richard said, tapping his forehead. "Think next time."

He opened the door of the shuttle and began to walk inside.

"We've been thinking **PLENTY!**" Starlight yelled.

Richard hesitated. "What do you mean?"

At that moment, DJ was able to free his arm and flung the puck high and far into the air.

The tardigrades turned and watched as the puck landed with a clack just in front of the now wide-open tardigrade goal, and **RIGHT AT THE FEET OF BENNY**.

Who, of course, no longer had a stick.

CHAPTER SEVENTEEN
IN SPACE NO ONE CAN HEAR YOUR TEAM

Rats," Jenny said.

"Ooops," said Benny.

The tardigrades were now **CHARGING BACK** into their end.

"Now what?" said Benny. "Can't kick in a goal. Won't count."

Before Jenny could respond, a tardigrade slammed into Benny and **SENT HIM FLYING**. Jenny reached out to him, but it was too late. Benny spun away, **OFF THE ASTEROID AND INTO SPACE.**

"**NOOOOOoOo!**" Jenny yelled. She tried to leap up to catch him, but he was **TOO FAR AWAY, MOVING TOO FAST**.

Benny twisted and turned, over and over, **GETTING SMALLER AND SMALLER** against the backdrop of a million stars.

Jenny looked back at the puck. The tardigrade net was just a few metres away, the goalie back between the posts. "**WHO CARES ABOUT THIS STUPID GAME?**" she said, tears in her eyes. She kicked the puck with the force of a missile.

It hit the tardigrade goalie in the stomach, then fell to the ice. The goalie stared at the disc, then back to Jenny. Jenny blinked the tears from her eyes and began skating as fast as she could toward the end boards, trying to get up enough speed to break free of the gravity of the asteroid. She tried again and again, but stayed rooted to the ice.

The other members of the Super Six were so shocked they couldn't move. Jenny, exhausted and angry, fell to the ice, sobbing.

The tardigrade goalie **STARED HARD AT JENNY,** growing more and more frustrated, then reached down and picked up the puck. Then it turned and **SLID THE PUCK INTO ITS OWN NET.**

"We win," DJ said, with zero joy.

THE TARDIGRADE GOALIE NODDED.

"WHAT **IS** HAPPENING?" Richard called.

"ATTACK, YOU WICKED WATER BEARS! ATTACK!"

The largest tardigrade shook its head, then blew its trumpet sound and dropped its stick to the ice. The others did the same.

The tardigrades went over to hug Jenny.

Starlight felt tears well up. "We were both wrong," she called up to the scientist. "It's not good enough to be brainy. Or to be brainy and brawny. **YOU ALSO NEED TO HAVE A HEART.**"

"Pathetic," Richard said.

And then the tardigrades did something no one expected. They grabbed Jenny by her arms and legs and, together, **FLUNG HER INTO THE VACUUM OF SPACE.**

CHAPTER EIGHTEEN
COLD COMFORT

Starlight watched as Jenny flew into space like a shot.

Richard howled. "HAHAHAHAHA! SEE! VIOLENT TO THE CORE. Now, my tardigrade terrors, do the same to the remaining members of the **SILLY SIX**."

"IT'S **SUPER** SIX," Karl said. **HE BLASTED A VOLLEY OF ICE AT RICHARD**, who was

quickly encased in a
frozen shell. But only
for a moment. There was
a low hum, and **THE ICE**
SHATTERED INTO A THOUSAND
PIECES, then melted onto the
platform.

Richard brushed a few droplets off his arms.
"**HEATED SPACE SUIT**. See, brains also defeat
your pitiful attempts at force. **NOW, GOODBYE,**
FOREVER."

He walked back into the shuttle, fired the rockets, and flew off, **LEAVING THE FOUR REMAINING MEMBERS OF THE SIX ALONE** with the creatures that had just sent two of their friends to their certain doom.

What he didn't tell them was that, buried under the ice, was a **GIANT BOMB**.

He pressed a red button, and a clock on the bomb **BEGAN TO COUNT DOWN FROM FIVE MINUTES.**

HOCKEY SUPER ~~SIX~~ FOUR

ALSO AVAILABLE
NOTHING.
THE END.
THANKS FOR JOINING US FOR THESE THRILLING ADVENTURES.
GOODBYE.

ACKNOWLEDGEMENTS

I'd like to thank my editor and art director, Anne Shone and Yvonne Lam, for making this series so fun to work on.

While it lasted anyway.

Seriously, how did you think this book was going to end?

There are two kids hurtling through space. Space can kill a person in a million ways, starting with sucking all the air out of your body in seconds flat!

There's a tin can being held together by chewing gum.

Rinks across the globe are being bulldozed.

Six tardigrades and four kids are stranded on an asteroid that's either going to blow up or crash into Earth.

Richard has won.

It's over.

No more.

FINI.

It would take a galactic-sized leap of faith to believe otherwise.

Do you believe?

REALLY?

Well, you have a choice.

Do you believe?

NO? Close the book and have a great life. And forget about ever playing hockey again. The rinks will be gone.

YES? TURN THE PAGE.

CHAPTER NINETEEN
YOU DO BELIEVE!

Jenny could make out the spinning form of her brother, lit by the distant sun.

Tossed by all the joined force of the tardigrades, she was actually **MOVING FASTER** than he was.

She could feel the cold of space begin to seep through her super-suit even as she gained on Benny.

"**STRETCH!**" she called, hoping that their communication link still worked this far away from each other.

Benny heard and **HE THREW OUT HIS ARMS AND**

LEGS IN A STAR PATTERN. Jenny needed to be absolutely precise, or she would miss him and keep spinning past. She'd only get one shot.

"**STRETCH MORE!**"

Benny did his best to reach farther, and **JENNY SNAGGED HIS LEFT HAND**, looping her glove around his wrist and **GRIPPING AS TIGHTLY AS IF HE WERE A HOCKEY STICK**.

"Hey, sis!" Benny said, smiling.

"Hey, bro."

He hugged her. "Just like always. Slower than me. Tsk-tsk."

She slugged him, and he almost flew away, but she kept her grip on him.

They continued to fly away from the asteroid and their friends.

"I guess there's **NO REAL WAY TO STOP OUT HERE**," Jenny said.

"Unless we hit something. I think **STARLIGHT CALLED IT INERTIA**,"* Benny said.

"Well, we're hurtling toward Earth, sort of. That's a good thing, right?"

"Starlight also talked about the dangers of re-entry without a spaceship to protect you."

Starlight had regaled them all with statistics about the heat caused by the friction of re-entering Earth's atmosphere.

Jenny was having some trouble recalling the exact details. "Starlight said something about speed and mass churning things up to . . . was it a hundred degrees?"

"I'm pretty sure it was a lot more than that,"

---

* Good memory, Benny! See Appendix D.

Benny said. "And much as I love these super hockey suits, I don't think they are THAT good."

"**SO I GUESS WE'RE GOING TO BURN UP?**" Jenny asked.

Benny shrugged. "Maybe. We might just fly past Earth and then spin away forever!"

"A happy thought."

"**WELL, AT LEAST WE'LL BE TOGETHER,**" he said.

She slugged him again.

Benny rubbed his shoulder. "Any chance we'll catch up to our hockey sticks? I could use a little practice."

"Dunno. They could be close." Jenny peered into the distance. She didn't see the sticks. But she did see one of the nearby stars . . . moving.

CHAPTER TWENTY

LAUNCH BREAK

Richard couldn't stop laughing as he flew away from HIELO-23B and back toward Earth.

He pushed a button and his monitor filled with images of more **HOCKEY RINKS BEING BLOWN UP, BULLDOZED, PULVERIZED INTO DUST**.

He checked his banking app and saw that gazillions of dollars were now flowing into his account.

HE'D WON. Well, of course he'd won. **HE WAS A GENIUS.** Without the weaknesses of, say, Clarence Crosscheck or that pesky Starlight kid, he'd been able to design a plan based on pure intellect.

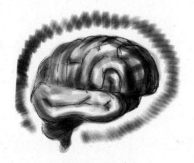

More importantly, **BRAINS** had won. Humanity might be sad for a while, but they'd come to thank him for **SAVING THEM FROM THE TYRANNY OF FUN**. How he hated that word.

By now the tardigrades had probably **JETTISONED THE REMAINING MEMBERS** of that horrible little hockey team into space. **OR CRUSHED THEM.**

If not, they'd all get blown up in — he checked the clock — four minutes. All the evidence of his experiments would be gone. Except for the knowledge that he'd been right.

Should he allow himself one small indulgence? Yes. He should.

He cut the power to his rockets and used boosters to turn and **WATCH AS HIELO-23B BLEW UP LIKE THE DEATH STAR**.

The only thing missing was, **"POPCORN!"**

He could almost smell the snack.

No, wait. The smell wasn't popcorn. It was . . . **ROASTED PEANUTS?**

CHAPTER TWENTY-ONE
EITHER ORBIT

The tardigrades watched the rocket blast away. Then they turned back to face the remaining members of the Hockey Super Six. Slowly, they began to lumber forward.

"**BACK OFF!**" DJ said, holding up the remains of his stick pathetically in front of him.

The tardigrade leader looked at the stick, then at DJ, then shook its head and stepped closer.

"It's gonna kill me," DJ said. "Just like it killed Benny and Jenny."

Mo crunched his knuckles. "**THOSE WERE OUR FRIENDS!**" he said. He got ready for the worst.

Karl raised his stick in the air, ready to fend off a tardigrade attack. He knew he wouldn't be able to do it for long, but he wasn't going to give up easily.

"Starlight," he said. "Any ideas?"

Starlight had been resting near the boards, **WATCHING JENNY SPIN AWAY.** She turned back around and gave a weak smile. "**DON'T WORRY, GUYS.**"

"Don't worry?" DJ's jaw dropped. "**ABOUT DYING?**"

"I've calculated the trajectory of Jenny's path. **THE TARDIGRADES DIDN'T TOSS HER INTO SPACE TO**

KILL HER, but to reunite her with her brother."

"By tossing her into space."

"Okay, yes, that is true. But, as I tried to tell Richard, it's because **THESE WONDERFUL CREATURES CARE, AS WELL AS THINK**."

"And crush," DJ said, waving at the remains of his equipment.

"I believe they are **STILL LEARNING** the limits of their strength and size. They've been up here alone for who knows how long. **THEY JUST WANTED TO PLAY.**"

The tardigrades nodded. Then they bowed their heads, looking contrite.

"Okay," DJ said, lowering his stick. "Maybe. But that still **DOESN'T HELP BENNY OR JENNY.**"

"Or help us figure out what to do to stop this asteroid from destroying Earth," Karl said.

All of a sudden, **THE TARDIGRADE GOALIE FELL TO THE ICE**, clutching its hands to its ears — or where the four presumed their ears were. The others fell down too, **MOANING AND TRUMPETING IN PAIN**.

"What's going on?" asked Karl.

In response, the goalie **POINTED AT CENTRE ICE**. It began punching, then let out a roar and clutched its ears again.

"THERE'S SOMETHING DOWN THERE!" Starlight said.

"On it," said Mo. He skated over and could see **A FAINT BLUE LIGHT BLINKING DEEP** under the ice.

He began pounding the surface with lightning speed. At first, nothing seemed to happen, then cracks began to appear. "A little help?"

DJ used the shaft of his stick to wedge huge chunks of ice free.

Starlight chipped.

Karl blasted.

It took about **THREE MINUTES**, but soon they'd dug a crater into the middle of the rink. **FROZEUM 7** dust covered them all and hung in the air.

Karl gathered it into a ball and threw it away, **REVEALING THE BOMB**. And on that bomb, a blue countdown clock read $1:00$.

Then $0:59$.

$0:58$ . . .

CHAPTER TWENTY-TWO
STAR STRUCK

O pen the pod bay door, Ron," Crosscheck said.

"We'll be sucked into space!" Ron said.

"Just do as I say!"

Ron looked at PM Patinage, who nodded. For better or worse, **THEY HAD TO TRUST CROSSCHECK**.

"Affirmative," Ron said. He walked over to the door and turned the handle. There was a puff of air and the door slid aside. He held the handle tightly as the vacuum of space began to suck out all the loose objects from the ship.

PM Patinage was held in place by her seatbelt, but she watched in horror as the material began to fray. "Whatever is going on, Crosscheck," she said. "Make it fast!"

Papers flew around, then out into the void of space. So did a lit paper bag filled with peanuts.

"Ooops," Crosscheck said.

"Ooops?" PM Patinage said.

"Why did I do this exactly?" Ron yelled, flapping like a flag in a hurricane.

Crosscheck smirked. "You'll see. Oh, and get ready to close the doors quickly."

"Quickly? **WHY?** OOFFF!!"

Ron said "OOFFF" because **SOMETHING HAD FLOWN INTO THE COCKPIT** and almost knocked him loose. He turned and saw a dark mass banging around the inside of the ship. It flew back toward him.

"CLOSE THE POD BAY DOOR NOW, RON!"

Ron struggled against the solar wind and pulled the door back into place. He locked the handle, then yelped as whatever the shape was slammed into his back, pinning him against the door.

CHAPTER TWENTY-THREE
PRO-PROPULSION

Mo continued to pound the ice, until the bomb itself came loose. **MO YANKED IT ONTO THE SURFACE.** He pulled back a fist, **READY TO PUNCH THE BOMB INTO SPACE.**

"**STOP!!!!**" Starlight yelled. "That's a percussion fuse on the side. Striking it will immediately **TRIGGER THE EXPLOSION!**"

0:30

"In thirty seconds, the BOMB is going to trigger the explosion!" Mo said.

The tardigrades were now blowing long slow blasts from their snouts. The countdown clock was clearly making a horrible noise only they could hear.

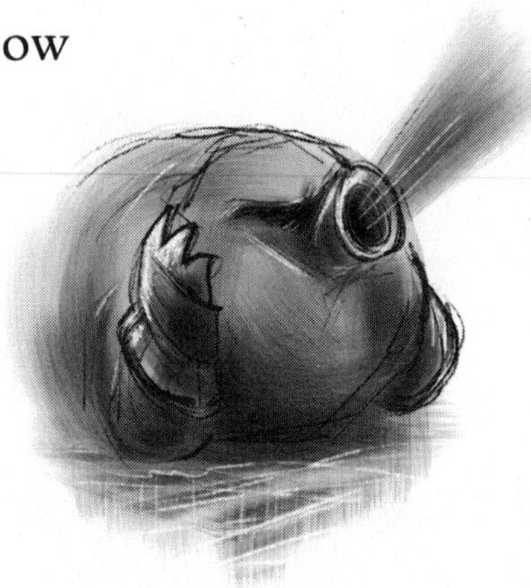

0:28

"I wish they'd stop doing that," Karl said. "I can't think."

"**SOUNDS LIKE DJ'S BUTT**," Mo joked.

0:27

"**DJ'S BUTT!**" Starlight said. "**THAT'S THE ANSWER!**"

"I can't deny it," DJ said.

0:25

"No, I mean, like you and your butt, **WE CAN USE PROPULSION TO SAVE OURSELVES AND, IF I'M RIGHT, EARTH.**"

0:22

"How?"

"There's no time to explain. Mo: Slide the bomb, carefully, as close to the edge of the asteroid as you can. Karl: Build a wall, a HUGE wall of ice, right in front of the bomb."

0:14

"In front?"

"NOW!"

Karl began constructing a wall of ice, dust, **FROZEUM 7** and bits of DJ's equipment in front of the bomb.

Starlight used her hands to estimate the angles. "A little more on the right," she said.

0:08

The bomb began to squeal loudly, and the kids got a taste of the pain the tardigrades were feeling.

0:05

Karl, exhausted, fell to the ice.

"**DOWN!**" Starlight yelled.

0:00

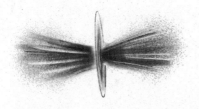

CHAPTER TWENTY-FOUR
MISSION CREEP

Richard shielded his eyes as a bright flash filled the window. It faded, and he lowered his hand. **THE BOMB HAD INDEED EXPLODED, EXACTLY AS HE'D TIMED IT.**

"Hmm. The debris field isn't as dramatic as I'd hoped. Still, can't argue with the results."

He coughed. **"ODD,"** he thought. The mysterious peanut smell was still there, and it had now been joined by an acrid odour. **"SMOKE?"**

A light flashed above his head. "Air quality

low, your intelligence," said a computerized voice that sounded a lot like his.

Richard flicked on the surveillance camera. A bag of peanuts, on fire, was **CLAMPED TIGHTLY AGAINST THE INTERIOR AIR FILTER.** "What the . . . ?"

Smoke was being sucked into the sealed environment of the ship. He coughed again as smoke filled the cabin.

"Delays, delays, delays." Richard lowered his visor, grabbed a broom, **OPENED THE SHUTTLE DOOR . . .** and found himself face to face with the **LAST PERSON HE'D EVER EXPECTED TO SEE.**

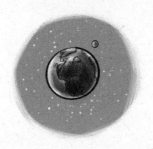

CHAPTER TWENTY-FIVE
NOW WHAT?

The high-pitched squeal was gone, and the tardigrades had stopped moaning. **OR WERE THEY ALL DEAD?** Karl wasn't sure.

Karl could feel the asteroid sway underneath him. He wasn't sure what Starlight's plan had been, but he **HOPED THIS WAS A SIGN IT HAD WORKED.**

He opened his eyes and pushed himself up.

The entire surface of the asteroid was **COVERED IN SHARDS OF ICE.** The tardigrades shook like dogs after a bath, sending bits of **FROZEUM 7** into the air. Mo and DJ were sitting back to back, picking bits of ice from their jerseys.

THEY WERE ALIVE!

The bomb had exploded, and his wall had cracked but held.

Starlight was sitting up, looking intensely at the stars.

"All good?" Karl asked, making his way over.

"The evidence appears to support the answer yes."

"So now that we did it . . . What did we do?"

"We essentially replicated DJ's save, at a larger scale, inside the capsule."

"But better smelling."

"Indeed. DJ had used a burst of gas to propel himself forward by a few millimetrers. **WE USED**

A SLIGHTLY LARGER BURST TO CHANGE THE TRAJECTORY OF HIELO-23B."

"How much did we change it by?" asked Mo, joining them.

Starlight pointed out toward the horizon.

"Before the blast, Earth was straight ahead." She swivelled her arm to the left. "Now it's there."

The others looked to where she was pointing.

"SO WE'RE NOT HEADING STRAIGHT FOR EARTH?" asked DJ.

"No. **WE SHOULD PASS BY.** A close call, but we did it."

"MY BUTT SAVES THE DAY AGAIN," DJ said. "Won't be the last time."

"Wait," Karl said. "Doesn't that mean we'll just **KEEP FLYING AWAY IN SPACE?"**

"FOREVER?" DJ asked.

Starlight nodded. **"BUT EARTH WILL BE SAFE."**

The tardigrades, somehow understanding what was going on, joined them and they all sat down together.

They sat in silence for a long time, watching the stars, watching Earth growing larger, but now safely out of their flight path.

"Hey," DJ said standing up. "I see a shooting star! Let's make a wish."

"There are no shooting stars in space," Starlight said. "They're caused by—"*

---

* You'll have to check Appendix E to find out why, because Starlight looked up to where DJ was pointing and, indeed, saw a shooting star heading straight for them.

CHAPTER TWENTY-SIX
SLINGSHOT EFFECT

Oh no!" Starlight said. "It's the Richard Rocket!"

"He's coming back to finish us off!" Karl said.

The tardigrades were up like a shot. They grabbed their sticks, ready to throw them like javelins.

The sleek blue shuttle slowed as it approached the asteroid, sending out puffs of mist as it steadied itself in a floating pattern just above the surface.

The door opened and **A SLIGHTLY RAGGED PYLON RICHARD APPEARED**, shuffling unsteadily onto the platform.

The tardigrades trumpeted so loud his hair moved, and they reared back to hurl their sticks.

"**WAIT!**" Karl yelled. "**LOOK! HE'S TIED UP!**"

And sure enough, they could see that Richard was **COMPLETELY TAPED UP** with hockey tape.

"But who taped up Richard?" Mo asked.

CLAReNCE CROSSCHECK's

smiling face appeared.

"Okay tardigrades, throw away," DJ said.

"WAIT!" yelled Karl again. "**HE'S NOT ALONE!**"

And sure enough, this time **RON, PM PATINAGE AND THE TWINS** appeared on the platform.

"Hey, guys," said Jenny

and Benny, waving and smiling.

The tardigrades lowered their sticks, and the stairs dropped onto the ice.

"What is going on?" asked Starlight. "**HOW IS THIS POSSIBLE?**"

Richard stumbled and fell, repeating the line, **"YES, HOW IS THIS POSSIBLE?"** over and over.

Crosscheck joined them on the surface and sat down on his captive rival. "It seems **you needed a GENIUS to defeat a genius**. I volunteered."

"Not exactly," said the Prime Minister. "Desperate times call for desperate measures, as they say. And he had a ship, of sorts."

Crosscheck stared into space. "Now just more interstellar debris, I'm afraid."

"Interplanetary actually," said Starlight. "There's **ONLY ONE STAR** in our solar system."

"Well, it almost took us with it!" said Ron.

The twins saw the look of confusion on their teammates' faces and filled them in about catching each other, the tin can rocket, and being caught by Crosscheck.

"Unfortunately my genius propulsion system was sacrificed in the manoeuver," Crosscheck said.

"A bag of burning peanuts . . ." Ron said.

"**An idea doesn't need to be COMPLEX to be genius.** I had saved the twins, but that left us unable to steer or change our path."

"Luckily that path took us right by Richard's shuttle," PM Patinage said. "So we, as they say, **HITCHED A RIDE**."

Benny beamed as he related how Crosscheck had made a tie-line from hockey tape and used

it to send Ron across the
distance between the ships. A
quick tape job on Richard, and
the rescue crew had a new and
slightly more high-tech ship.

Everyone, including the
tardigrades (but not including Crosscheck or
Richard) . . . okay, **ALMOST** everyone gathered for
a group hug.

"Well, Super Six," PM Patinage said. "Whaddya
say we head back home?"

The Six looked back at their new friends, the

tardigrades, who were waving goodbye and putting their hockey equipment back on.

"We can't just leave them here," Starlight said.

"They'll never fit inside that capsule," PM Patinage said.

The Six shuffled their feet, unsure what to do.

Crosscheck gave a little cough. "If I may . . . I have an idea. **But it will COST you.**"

CHAPTER TWENTY-SEVEN
STELLAR LUNAR

Bobby Orrbit spat out his powdered tuna sandwich shake as he stared in disbelief at the night sky.

Being the night security guard at the `GUMPP MOON` base was usually quiet. But this was the **SECOND JOLT** he'd had **THIS WEEK**.

The first had been a blinding laser beam that had made him spit out his "pepperoni pizza" all over his computer keyboard.

Now, this latest dinner was lost due to what

appeared to be a flying disc, spinning straight toward the lunar surface at incredible speed.

He flipped a switch with **RED ALERT** on top, and sirens began wailing. About a dozen people in GUMPP pyjamas stormed into the control room, arguing about what to do.

"What is that?"

"I THINK IT'S AN ASTEROID."

"Should we blow it up?"

"The space laser isn't ready yet."

(Clearly they hadn't read chapter two.)

"Oh yeah. We better alert the Prime Minister!"

Bobby nodded. He'd already begun calling PM Patinage on the `SUPER-SECRET GUMPP TELECOM LINE`. It rang a few times, then there was a click.

"PM Patinage here."

"PM PP," said Bobby. "We have a **SITUATION** on the Moon."

"A large asteroid is about to slam into the dark side? Shaped a little like a pizza?"

Someone behind PM Patinage chuckled, and she said, "Shhhhh," then turned back to the mouthpiece. "Thanks for the call, but it's all good."

Bobby took a few seconds to absorb what he'd just heard. "Are you saying you **WANT** the asteroid **TO SLAM INTO THE MOON?**"

It wasn't **UNHEARD** of. The Moon gets hit a lot,* and actually acts as a kind of protective shield for Earth. But this asteroid was **REALLY** big.

"Just take a look again," PM Patinage said.

And when Orrbit looked up again, he could see

---

* See Appendix F.

what looked like rocket blasts firing off the front and side of the rock. With each blast, the asteroid tilted and slowed, until it landed on the surface with a giant puff of lunar dust.

Orrbit had to **ZOOM IN** the security camera to believe it. He was shocked again as he saw what appeared to be a **LARGE HOCKEY RINK, SIX CHILDREN AND SIX ELEPHANTS . . . PLAYING HOCKEY?**

There was a knock at the door. Orrbit opened the airlock. Prime Minister Pauline Patinage walked in, followed by the strangest-looking goalie Orrbit had ever seen, and a furious mummy.

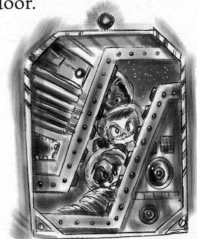

EPILOGUE

Mo scarfed down his tenth slice of pizza. "**THIS PIZZA LOOKS LIKE AN ASTEROID,**" he said.

"You think everything looks like an asteroid," DJ joked.

Mo smiled and moved on to slices eleven and twelve and beyond.

Karl munched happily on some mushroom bruschetta. "You notice how food tastes better when you enjoy it in a nice setting?"

The Six were sitting inside their new hangout, which was definitely nice. Their locker room had been damaged by the earthquake. This new one had been the head office of the Richard Corporation, `NOW PROPERTY OF GUMPP`.

PM Patinage's face appeared on the huge HDTV, pausing the game of *PUCKS OF GLORY 7* between DJ and Starlight.

"It's nice to see you all taking some time to relax," PM PP said.

"I think we've earned a little downtime," Karl said.

"Nice of Richard to leave behind all of this **TOP-NOTCH STUFF**," DJ grinned, holding up his video game controller and VR helmet.

PM Patinage nodded. "Well, it's the least we could do to thank you all for **ALMOST DYING**. And since Richard is being kept safely in our high-security Moon base prison, **IT'S FREE FOR YOU TO ENJOY**."

"**SO, HOW'S CLARENCE?**" asked the twins. They were sitting in the built-in hot tub, sipping hot chocolates piled high with whipped cream.

"**CLARENCE?**" Starlight raised an eyebrow.

Jenny shrugged. "When a guy saves you from hurtling forever in space, it kinda brings you closer, you know?"

"Crosscheck is back in his cell," PM Patinage said. "But, according to his demands, we have rebuilt the Penticton Double Trouble Rinkarama, and will allow him to practise there once a week — with a full cadre of **ARMED ROBOT GUARDS** of course."

"I kind of figured he'd ask for more," Starlight said. "He did save Earth, AND us, AND helped save the tardigrades from drifting away forever."

"I know," said PM Patinage. "But **HE SEEMED EAGER TO RETURN TO HIS OLD CELL.** Oh well. Mysteries for a later date."

"How are the big space puppies doing?" asked Mo.

"The tardigrades are actually an unexpected bonus for the staff at the Moon base," PM Patinage glared at DJ. "The Moon base that does **NOT** exist."

"Right," DJ winked. "Gotcha."

Ron displayed video of the new Moon base rink, complete with lights. "They play the staff there in some, I'm told, **VERY ENTERTAINING** games."

"Three tardigrades a side," said PM Patinage. "To keep it fair."

The camera followed Bobby Orrbit being **HIP CHECKED HIGH IN THE AIR** and then landing with a puff of dust in a shallow crater.

"It helps that the gravity on the Moon makes for a slightly softer landing," Ron said.

"The hockey also helps deal with the monotony," said PM Patinage. "And . . . they broadcast the games on a TV in Richard's cell. In case he has a change of heart."

"Or mind," said Starlight bitterly.

"We **NEVER DID SCORE A REAL GOAL** against those big lugs," Karl said, shaking his head.

"Yeah. Just imagine if they ever get turned evil and challenge us to a life-or-death game!" said the twins. "We'd get our **BUTTS KICKED**."

DJ laughed. "**BUTTS**."

PM Patinage clapped her hands. "Anyway, things have settled down for now. I've got some pre-election business to attend to. And while we take a few weeks to rebuild the hockey rinks, **I HAVE ONE ORDER I NEED YOU TO FOLLOW**."

"What's that?" asked the Six.

"**A VERY SHORT BREAK FROM HOCKEY**."

The twins almost leaped out of the tub. "**IMPOSSIBLE!**" they said.

"Whoa, whoa." PM Patinage held up her hands. "Look. There's a shortage of rinks right now, and there are kids out there who need some ice time."

The twins crossed their arms. "So do we."

"And Starlight can back me up on this. Numerous studies show that **PLAYING A VARIETY OF SPORTS IS ACTUALLY BETTER FOR YOU.**"*

The twins glared at Starlight. "Better how?"

"It is true," Starlight said. "I can cite the studies if you'd like."

"Give us the short version," said the twins.

"Well, the bottom line is that if your goal is to become truly better at hockey, then **PLAYING OTHER SPORTS IS HIGHLY RECOMMENDED.** It exercises different muscles, and also sparks different parts of your brain."

---

* See Appendix G if you don't believe her.

"Are you saying **WE** need to get better at **HOCKEY?**"

Starlight calmly pointed back at the image of the tardigrades playing against the GUMPP Moon base staff.

"WANT TO ACTUALLY BEAT THESE GUYS SOMEDAY?"

"Good point," said the twins sheepishly.

PM Patinage jumped in. "Ron has some schedules for all the various sports camps."

Ron handed the kids pamphlets.

"Ohhh!" Mo said. **"I'VE ALWAYS WANTED TO TRY BASKETBALL."**

"Me too," said Starlight. They high-fived.

The twins looked at each other and grinned. "You didn't tell us there's such a thing as **DOUBLES**

TENNIS! We're in!"

"How about you, Karl and DJ," asked Starlight.

"Well," said Karl, "as soon as my mom hangs up on this call, DJ and I are going to get back to some good old **E-GAMING**."

DJ nodded. "Which I will then win."

"Then we're agreed," said PM Patinage. "Enjoy. And let's hope we all have a few quiet weeks to rest and relax and **TRY SOME NEW EXPERIENCES**."

She hung up.

Mo and Starlight began passing a basketball.

The twins were holding their tennis racquets like hockey sticks.

"I think you might need some tips," Ron said.

"There are basketball and tennis courts on the roof."

He led four of the six away.

Karl and DJ continued blasting electronic pucks at each other.

The only thing neither had noticed was that the virtual reality headsets they'd put on had an **ALMOST MICROSCOPIC** manufacturer's label.

IT READ . . .

MANUFACTURED IN CANADA.
BY CPPMUG INDUSTRIES.

THE END?

APPENDICES

Appendix A

Yes, there are fault lines running through the entire country. The Mattawa and Petawawa Faults run mostly east-west near Ottawa, and result in a number of earthquakes each year. You can also look up the "Ottawa-Bonnechere Graben" for more information about how the fault lines got there. Hint: tectonic plates.

Appendix B

Mount Logan is indeed growing each year, by a tiny amount. Why? Hint: tectonic plates. These are huge parts of the Earth's crust that are constantly moving. They form mountains slowly, but keep pushing up as they push against each other.

Appendix C

Astronauts have done lots of fun things in space. Canadian Chris Hadfield played guitar. Sometimes they make pizza, or put on Halloween masks to scare their friends. And sometimes they play hockey. Well, sort of. Astronauts have brought small plastic sticks and pucks into space and played a mini version of the game. It's not easy controlling a floating puck!

Appendix D

Inertia basically means that an object in motion (Benny and Jenny) will keep moving in a straight line unless something external (a wall, gravity) acts on them. In space, there are only a few things like that, and they are waaaaaaaaayyyy far apart. So an object moving in one direction tends to stay in that direction.

Appendix E

Shooting stars are, of course, not stars. They are bits of dust, rock and ice that crash toward Earth from space. We have an atmosphere that they have to pass through. The friction causes them to heat up and burn. It's a great light show!

Appendix F

If you see close-up images of the Moon, you notice it is COVERED in craters. Those are caused by bits of space rock smashing into the Moon. Little ones hit every day, and hundreds of larger bits smash into the surface every year. It's a good thing too, because that stops some of those rocky bits from hitting Earth.

Appendix G

Your body has a lot of different muscles. If you play only one sport, that tends to work one set of muscles. That increases the chances of injury and fatigue — wearing out that one set of muscles and not activating the rest.

And some skills from one sport can help you in ways you might not expect. The hand-eye coordination needed to play tennis can help you spot the puck as a hockey player. Guarding an opponent in basketball is a great way to practise finding your centre of gravity, and pivoting and changing directions quickly.

Then there's the mental side of things. Doing any one thing over and over and over can become tiresome and, well, boring. So coaches, trainers and sports organizations are pretty unanimous in encouraging trying a lot of different sports to make you better at them all.

HOCKEY SUPER SIX

ALSO AVAILABLE

THE PUCK DROPS HERE
ON THIN ICE
HAT TRICKED

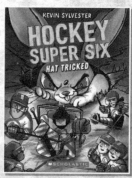